For Anne — RM, SM

To all the people who work tirelessly to advocate for orphaned or injured animals in the wild; to the Qalipu Mi'kmaq First Nation, stewards of the land and sea in and around Seal Cove; to all those who contributed to the rescue of the dolphins at Seal Cove; and to the Hope for Wildlife Society—JF

Roy Miki & Slavia Miki

DOLPHIN SOS

Illustrations by

Julie Flett

Afterword by Richard Cannings

Tradewind Books

VANCOUVER · LONDON

I was awakened, not by the whistling of the wind nor the strong gusts rattling my bedroom window. I had heard those sounds before. This time the sounds were more piercing, more eerie.

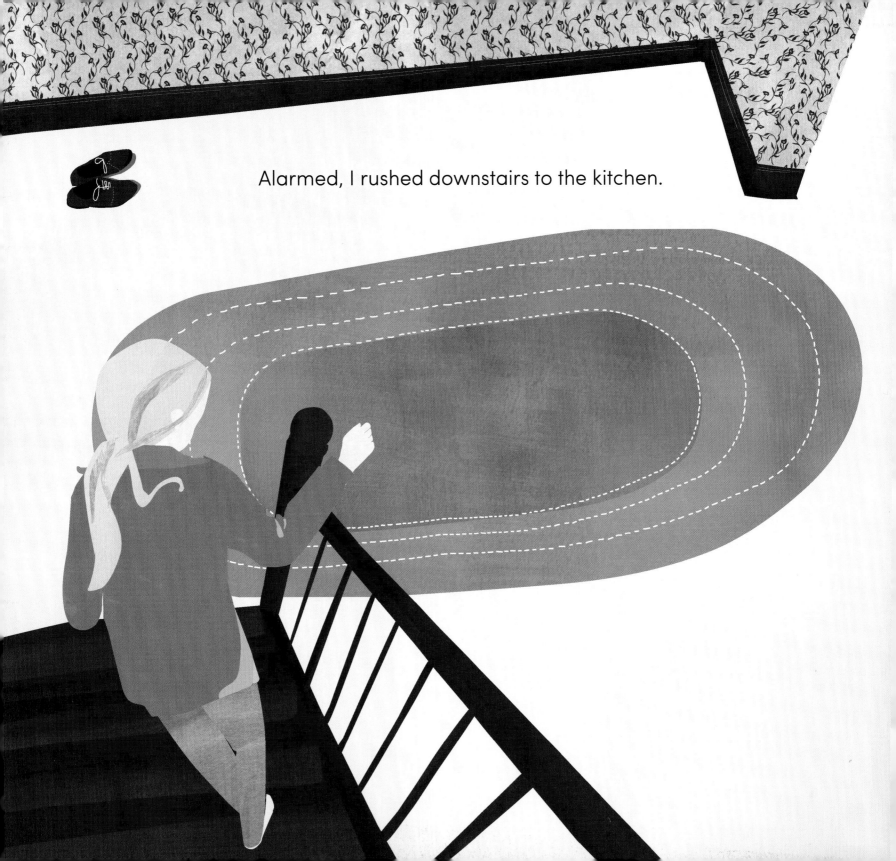

Alarmed, I rushed downstairs to the kitchen.

"Mom, what are those scary sounds?"

"They're dolphins, Nicole. They've been crying for hours. The storm blew in large sheets of ice, trapping them in the cove."

"Where's Aaron?"

"He's down there with Patrick."

"I'm going too!"

I put on my warmest coat, boots and scarf, and hurried down to the cove. The snow was still falling, and the swirling wind stung my face.

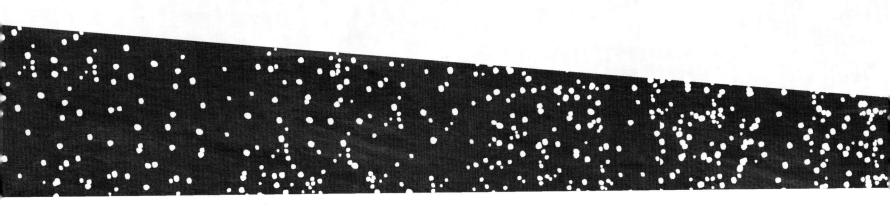

Three dolphins were circling in a small patch of water. Their shrill cries rang out as they hit their heads against the ice, trying to break free.

"It's terrible!" I cried. "They're sending out an SOS! Why don't we help them?"

"We asked a government official to send an icebreaker, but there wasn't one on hand," answered Aaron.

"What can we do?"

"There's nothing we can do. We were told that we had to let nature take its course."
But then the dolphins will die.
I went home with the dolphins' desperate cries ringing in my ears.

For three days and three nights the dolphins' mournful wails echoed through the town.

SOS! SOS! SOS!

I tossed and turned in my bed.

No one could sleep, not even the cats and dogs.

The ice closed in on the dolphins.

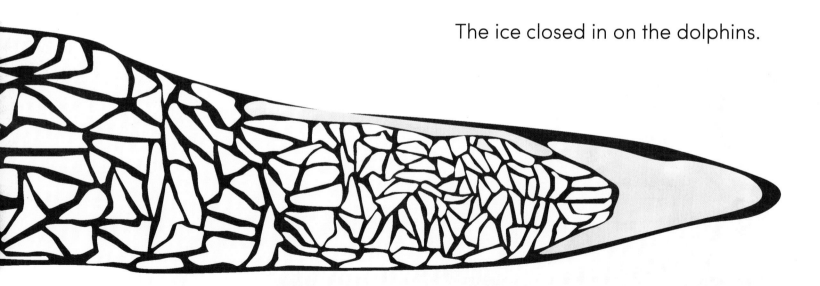

SOS! SOS! SOS!

Aaron, Patrick and I watched the dolphins thrash about helplessly.

  "Soon they won't have enough space to stay afloat and breathe," I said. "They'll drown!"

  "Never mind about letting nature take its course," Aaron said. "We have to do something."

"Want to go for a swim?" Patrick's eyes twinkled.
"I've got survival suits in the truck."
Aaron's face lit up. "We need help."
"Can I come too?" I asked.
"You're too young," my brother said.

Disappointed, I rushed home to get my binoculars.

I joined the crowd gathering on the road that overlooked the cove, adjusted my binoculars, and watched.

I hope it's not too late.

Aaron stood on the ice wearing his survival suit. Patrick and three men got into a small boat, and working together they rocked it back and forth for five hours. Inch by inch, they slowly broke a path to the open sea.

Two of the dolphins followed the boat to freedom, but the third one didn't have the strength. She had deep cuts on her body and struggled to keep her head above water.

Don't give up, I thought.

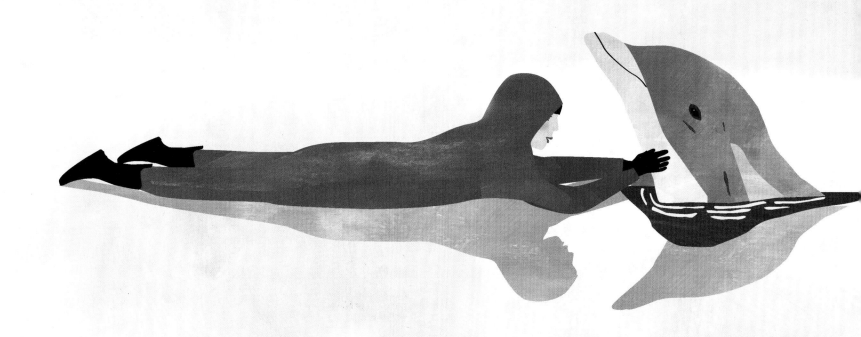

Aaron stretched himself out flat on his belly
and crawled toward the dolphin. He
reached out his hand and stroked her head.
 The dolphin stopped crying.

Then Aaron slipped into the water and put his arms around her. She wrapped her fins around his waist. Aaron rubbed his hands over her slick, rubbery face. She no longer struggled, trusting Aaron's touch.

Aaron looked into the dolphin's dark, watery eyes.

She looked back into his.

They held each other for an hour, Aaron's survival suit keeping them afloat.

The men returned from guiding the other dolphins into open water.

Patrick tossed Aaron a rope. Aaron tied it around the injured dolphin to create a harness, and climbed into the boat. Together they pulled her to safety.

After they removed the harness, a miraculous change occurred. The dolphin came to life, slowly swimming in circles as she regained her strength.

The dolphin swam out to the open sea three times, only to return each time to the boat.

The dolphin is thanking them for saving her life, I thought.

But then, with a high dancing leap and a splash of her tail, the dolphin turned, winked at *me*, and swam out to sea.

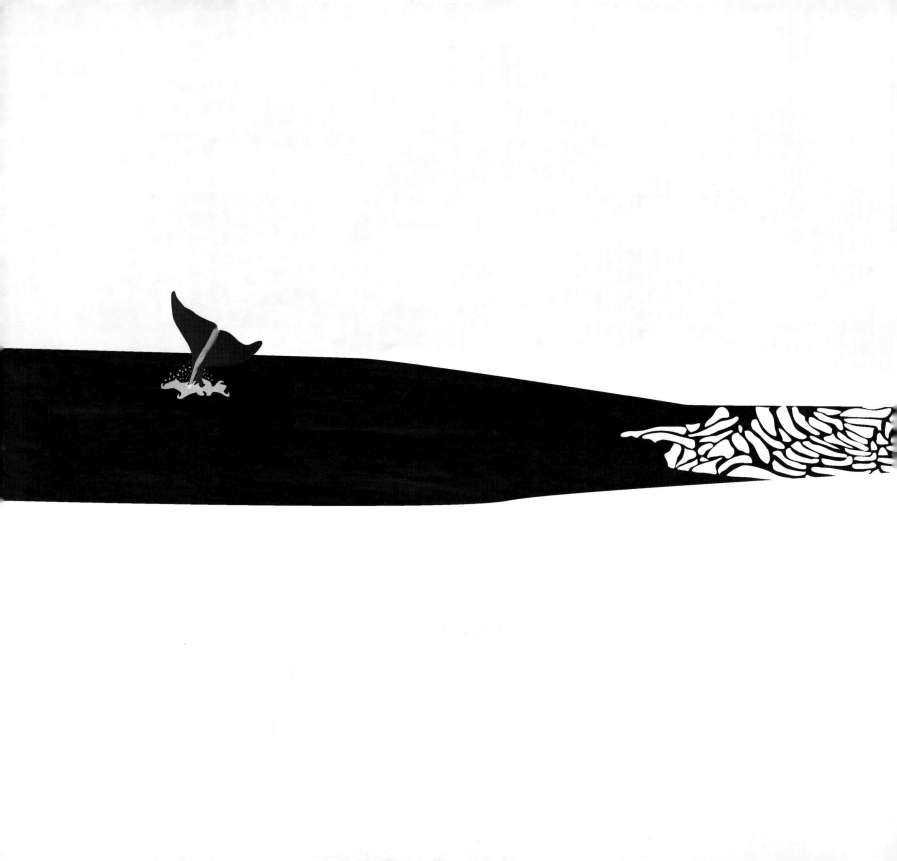

Mayor Vince congratulated the tired rescue team. "It's a beautiful ending," he said.

Wrapping my arms around Aaron, I whispered, "Thank you for answering the dolphins' SOS."

"Yes, SOS. It was the right thing to do." Aaron winked.

WHITE-BEAKED DOLPHIN

Richard Cannings

The dolphins in this story are white-beaked dolphins—one of about 70 species of dolphins and porpoises found around the world.

Adult white-beaked dolphins are about nine metres long and weigh between 180 and 350 kilograms—two or three times the weight of a grown man. They are found in the north Atlantic Ocean, from the limit of the Arctic ice south to Great Britain and Nova Scotia. Several thousand live around Newfoundland and Labrador.

White-beaked dolphins hunt for schools of fish in relatively shallow waters, swimming rapidly in small groups or pods. Sometimes a group of dolphins will herd a school of fish into a circle and trap them against the surface. They use echolocation, a kind of underwater radar, to find fish by making loud clicking noises with their blowholes. When the sound waves hit a school of fish, they are reflected back to the dolphins, who hear the sound through vibrations that pass up their jaws to their ears.

Because they hunt in coastal waters, white-beaked dolphins can be corralled by ice movements or beached at low tide.

• • •

RICHARD CANNINGS *is a biologist and author living in Penticton, BC, where he organizes continent-wide bird surveys and writes popular books on natural history. His mother's family came to BC from Harbour Grace, Newfoundland, so he shares a connection to the ice-bound bays of that island.*

ACKNOWLEDGEMENTS

Dolphins' SOS is a fictional story based on actual events. In February 2009, at Seal Cove, a small town of 250 on the Newfoundland west coast, five white-beaked dolphins became trapped by ice in White Bay. When community members, including Mayor Winston May, asked the Fisheries Department of the Canadian federal government for help, they were flatly turned down. They were warned that any intervention on their part would violate government regulations. For the Seal Cove residents, the daily sight of the struggling dolphins and the sound of their haunting cries were heart wrenching, especially for the children. The crisis point came on February 19 when it appeared that the dolphins would no longer survive. Roger Gavin, frustrated by the government's inaction, asked his friend, 16-year-old Brandon Banks, to help clear a channel to open water. Ruben Giles, Rodney Rice, and Melvin Rice joined them. When the men arrived in Roger's fiberglass boat, they found only three dolphins. Two dolphins had made their way to open water. There was no evidence to suggest otherwise.

Roger, Brandon, Ruben, Rodney and Melvin worked for five hours to open a path 400 metres in length for the dolphins. Two dolphins followed their boat to freedom, but the third one was too weak to swim. Brandon stayed with this dolphin in the small hole, keeping it afloat. When the men returned, he harnessed the dolphin. When taken to open water, the dolphin amazingly regained its strength. Once freed, it returned to the boat three times before swimming away on its own, as if to acknowledge what the men had done.

News of the rescue drew a multitude of tributes from around the world. Brandon and the four men were rightfully hailed as heroes. Slavia and I were deeply touched by their compassionate spirit that affirmed the responsibility we all have to alleviate the suffering of living beings in need. In writing *Dolphins' SOS*, we wish to honour these men and the people of Seal Cove for their courage in answering the SOS call.

Our sincere thanks to those who shared their accounts of the rescue: Doreen and Roger Gavin in phone conversations; Ruben Giles, Rodney Rice and Brandon Banks, the members of the rescue team available during Roy's visit to Seal Cove; Lydia Banks, Brandon's mother; Winston May, the mayor of Seal Cove. Jean Young provided invaluable assistance in driving Roy and his friends, Smaro Kamboureli and Larissa Lai, from Deer Lake to Seal Cove on a truly memorable highway journey. Finally, our thanks to Michael Katz for excellent editorial feedback and advice.

This story is dedicated to Slavia's mother, Anne, who always opened her heart to animals in distress.

Published by Tradewind Books in Canada and the UK in 2014
Text copyright © 2014 Roy Miki and Slavia Miki
Illustrations copyright © 2014 Julie Flett

LIBRARY AND ARCHIVES CANADA CATALOGUING IN PUBLICATION

Miki, Roy, 1942-, author
    Dolphin SOS / written by Roy and Slavia Miki ; illustrated by
Julie Flett ; afterword by Richard Cannings.

ISBN 978-1-896580-76-0 (bound)

    1. Dolphins--Juvenile fiction. 2. Animal rescue--Juvenile fiction.
I. Miki, Slavia, 1943-, author II. Flett, Julie, illustrator III. Title.

PS8576.I32D64 2014   jC813'.54   C2013-907594-1

Cataloguing and publication data available from the British Library

Book design by Elisa Gutiérrez

The type is set in Sofia Pro. Title type is The Hand.

10   9   8   7   6   5   4   3   2   1

Printed and bound in Korea in May 2014 by Sung In Printing Company.

Tradewind Books wishes to thank Shed Simas and Meaghan Hall for their
editorial help with this project.

The publisher thanks the Government of Canada and Canadian Heritage
for their financial support through the Canada Council for the Arts, the
Canada Book Fund and Livres Canada Books. The publisher also thanks
the Government of the Province of British Columbia for the financial support
it has given through the Book Publishing Tax Credit program and the British
Columbia Arts Council.